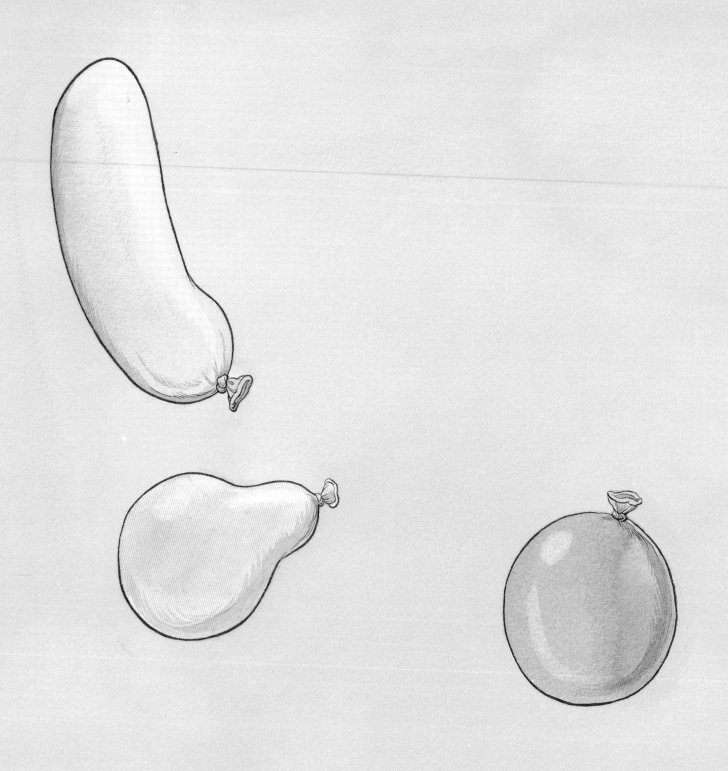

PUFFIN BOOKS

Published by the Penguin Group
Penguin Books Ltd, 80 Strand, London WC2R 0RL, England
Penguin Group (USA), Inc., 375 Hudson Street, New York, New York 10014, USA
Penguin Books Australia Ltd, 250 Camberwell Road, Camberwell, Victoria 3124, Australia
Penguin Books Canada Ltd, 10 Alcorn Avenue, Toronto, Ontario, Canada M4V 3B2
Penguin Books India (P) Ltd, 11 Community Centre, Panchsheel Park, New Delhi – 110 017, India
Penguin Books (NZ) Ltd, Cnr Rosedale and Airborne Roads, Albany, Auckland, New Zealand
Penguin Books (South Africa) (Pty) Ltd, 24 Sturdee Avenue, Rosebank 2196, South Africa

Penguin Books Ltd, Registered Offices: 80 Strand, London WC2R 0RL, England

www.penguin.com

First published in hardback 2003
First published in paperback 2004
1 3 5 7 9 10 8 6 4 2

Copyright © Chris Riddell, 2003
All rights reserved

The moral right of the author/illustrator has been asserted

Set in Monotype Poliphilus

Manufactured in China

British Library Cataloguing in Publication Data
A CIP catalogue record for this book is available from the British Library

ISBN 0–140–56779–8

Platypus and the Birthday Party

CHRIS RIDDELL

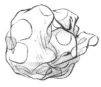

PUFFIN

Platypus gave Bruce a big hug.
"Happy birthday, Bruce," he said. "Birthdays
only come once a year and I know just how
to make this one very special for you."

Platypus found a box at the back of his cupboard. It had everything he needed inside.

Party hats ...   decorations ...   and games.

Now, thought Platypus. What else do I need
for Bruce's birthday party?
I know. Guests! I'll invite Echidna.
"ECK-KID-NAH," he said,
writing her name
carefully in his
best handwriting.

"Did I hear my name?" said a soft voice.

"Echidna!" said Platypus, smiling. "I was just inviting you to Bruce's birthday party."

"Oh good," said Echidna. "I love birthday parties."

"What a beautiful hat," she said.

"I made this one for you,"
said Platypus proudly,
putting it on her head.

"Thank you," said
Echidna, blushing.
"But where is
the cake?"
"Cake?" said Platypus.

"Yes," said Echidna. "You can't have a birthday party without a cake."
So Platypus and Echidna got everything they needed and mixed it all up in a big bowl.

Then they put the cake on a plate.

"What are we missing?" asked Platypus.

"I know," said Echidna. "Bananas!"

"Of course," said Platypus.

"That's great, but what is it?" asked Platypus.
"It's an Echidna cake! Do you think Bruce
will like it?" she said shyly.
"Bruce will love it," said Platypus.

"Now, how about balloons?" said Echidna.

"Balloons?" said Platypus.

"Yes," said Echidna quietly, "you've got to have balloons."

Platypus rummaged in his special box.

"Will these do?" he said.

"Perfect," said Echidna, smiling.

Platypus tried to blow
up the red balloon.

It flew out of his beak
and made a rude noise.

"I'm not very good at
balloon blowing," he sighed.

"Let me try," said Echidna.
She took a deep breath
and blew …

and blew …

and blew …

"Let's play!"

said Platypus.

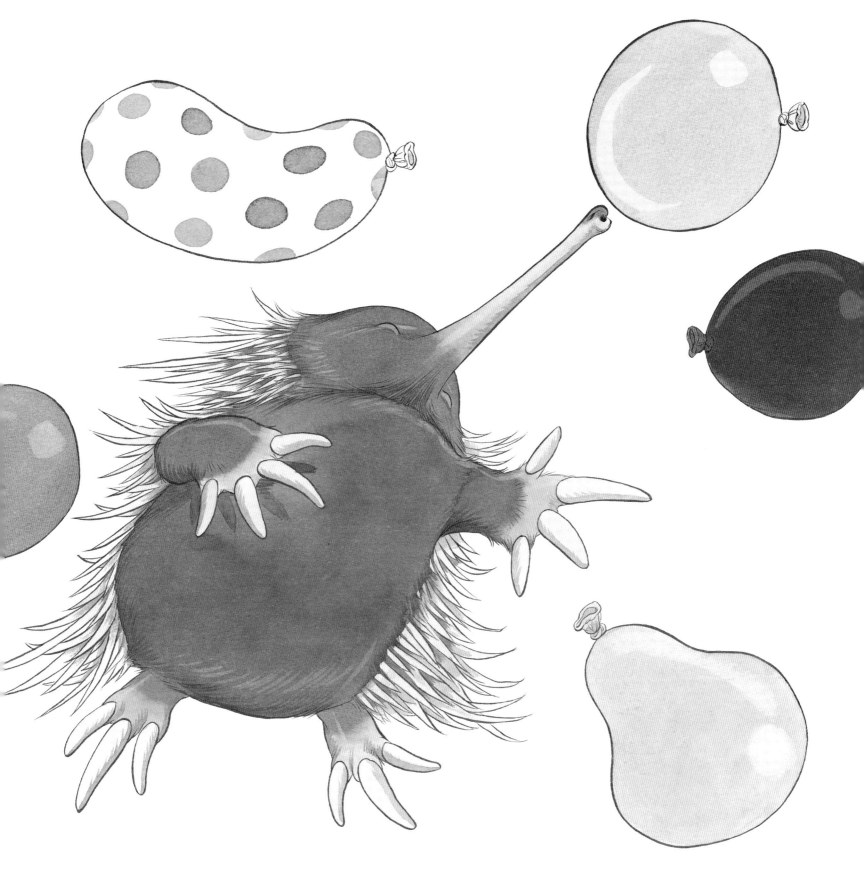

"I'm not very good at playing with balloons," said Echidna. "That's all right," said Platypus. "Let's make some paper chains."

Platypus and Echidna set to work.

They were *both* good at making paper chains.

At last everything was ready. They took the paper
chains, the decorations, the games and the cake outside.
"Is that everything?" asked Echidna.
"I think so," said Platypus.

"Bruce!" said Platypus, running inside.
"We can't have the birthday party without Bruce."

Happy Birthday to you!

Platypus carried
Bruce on his comfy
cushion. And Echidna
and Platypus sang
"Happy Birthday".

Happy Birthday to you!

"Thank you for your help, Echidna," said Platypus.
"You're welcome," said Echidna.
"I love birthdays."
"I do too," said Platypus.
"Let's have another
one tomorrow."

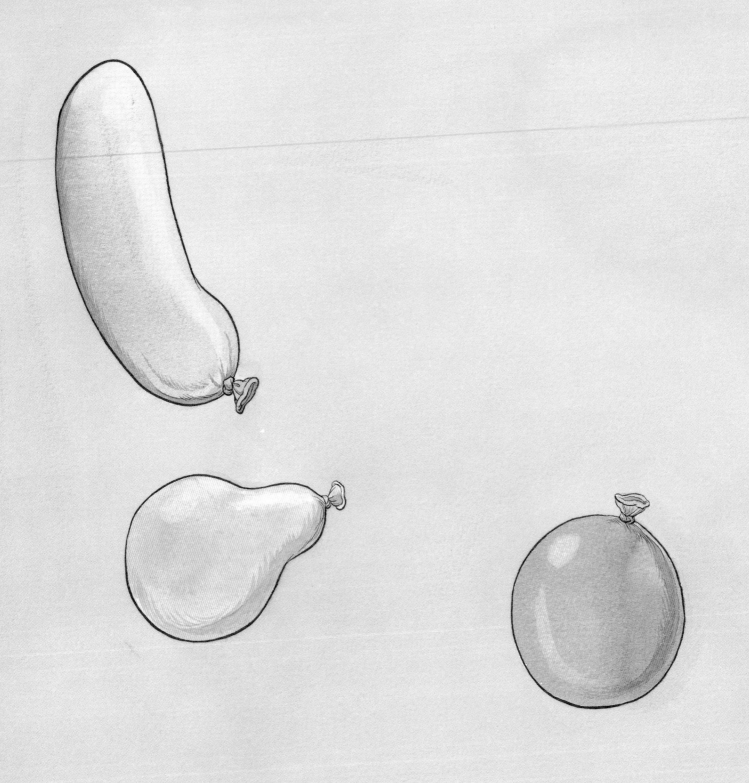